KAREN LATCHANA KENNEY

THE SCIENCE OF
STARS

EXPLORING MATTER

Checkerboard
Library

An Imprint of Abdo Publishing
abdopublishing.com

3 9082 13140 7614

abdopublishing.com

Published by Abdo Publishing, a division of ABDO, PO Box 398166, Minneapolis, Minnesota 55439. Copyright © 2016 by Abdo Consulting Group, Inc. International copyrights reserved in all countries. No part of this book may be reproduced in any form without written permission from the publisher. Checkerboard Library™ is a trademark and logo of Abdo Publishing.

Printed in the United States of America, North Mankato, Minnesota

102015
012016

 THIS BOOK CONTAINS RECYCLED MATERIALS

Design: Christa Schneider
Production: Mighty Media, Inc.
Editor: Liz Salzmann

Cover Photos: Shutterstock, front cover, back cover
Interior Photos: ITAR-TASS Photo Agency/Alamy, p. 9; Library of Congress, p. 19; NASA, pp. 13, 20, 26; Shutterstock, pp. 6, 7, 8, 10, 11, 12, 14, 15, 16, 17, 18, 21, 22, 23, 24, 25, 27, 28, 29; Wikimedia Commons, 19

Library of Congress Cataloging-in-Publication Data

Kenney, Karen Latchana, author.
  The science of stars : exploring matter / by Karen Latchana Kenney.
     pages cm. -- (Science in action)
  Includes index.
  ISBN 978-1-62403-965-2
1. Stars--Structure--Juvenile literature. 2. Matter--Properties--Juvenile literature. 3. Matter--Constitution--Juvenile literature. I. Title.
  QB808.K46 2016
  523.8'6--dc23
                          2015026278

CONTENTS

A NEW STAR!

Deep in space, a dust cloud churns. Tiny specks of matter move in gases. The mass swells in one spot. The dust and gases gather together. They collapse under their gravity. The pressure makes a hot **core**.

4

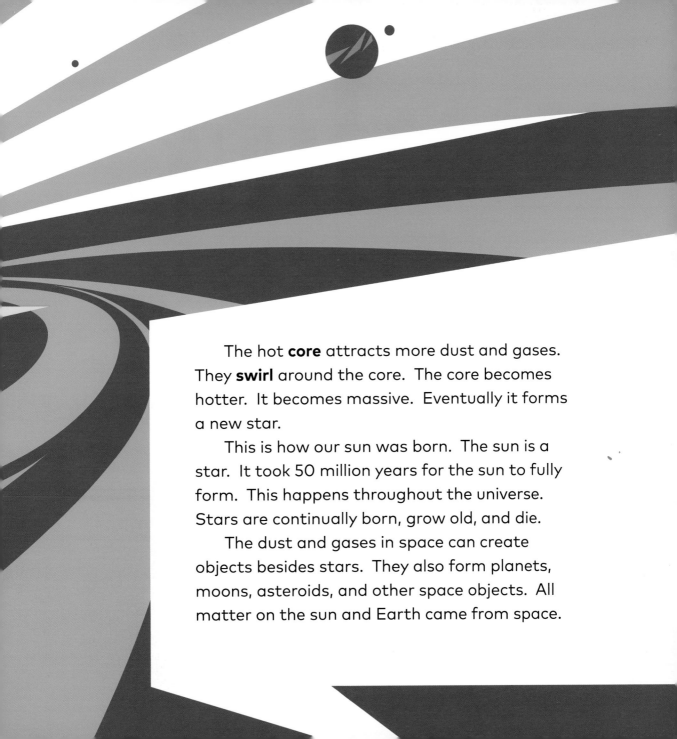

The hot **core** attracts more dust and gases. They **swirl** around the core. The core becomes hotter. It becomes massive. Eventually it forms a new star.

This is how our sun was born. The sun is a star. It took 50 million years for the sun to fully form. This happens throughout the universe. Stars are continually born, grow old, and die.

The dust and gases in space can create objects besides stars. They also form planets, moons, asteroids, and other space objects. All matter on the sun and Earth came from space.

WHAT IS MATTER?

CHAPTER 1

Everything is made of matter. It fills the air you breathe. It is the water in the ocean. It is what your body is made out of. It is what plants are made out of too.

Small particles of matter form atoms. An atom is the basic unit of a chemical element. Atoms combine to make molecules. Groups of atoms and molecules make up everything in our world.

All matter has mass and takes up space. Some matter you can see and touch, like this book. Other matter is harder to see, like oxygen. Different kinds and forms of matter are found on Earth.

Everything you eat is made of matter.

MEASURING MATTER

RULER
Used for measuring length

SCALE
Used for measuring weight

BEAKER
Used for measuring volume

Not all matter can be measured in the same way. Different types of matter require different tools to measure them. Here are some tools scientists use to measure matter.

Solid matter can be measured with a ruler. Or it can be weighed on a scale. Other matter is in liquid form. It has to be measured in a container, such as a beaker.

7

SMALL
MATTER

Atoms are the basic parts of matter. An atom has a central nucleus. Inside the nucleus are protons and neutrons. Electrons orbit the nucleus.

The nucleus has a positive electrical charge. Electrons have a negative charge. Because of these opposing charges, the nucleus attracts the electrons.

A carbon atom

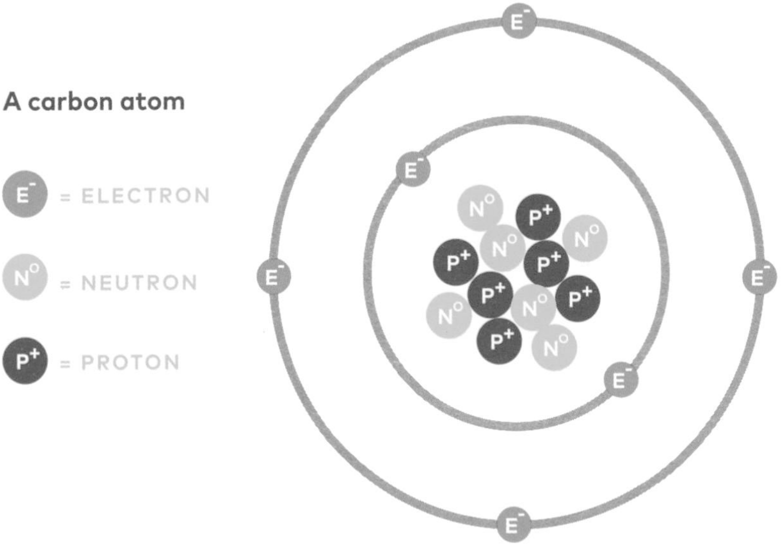

E^- = ELECTRON

N^0 = NEUTRON

P^+ = PROTON

This force keeps the electrons from floating away.

Each atom belongs to a chemical element. Atoms with the same number of protons belong to the same element. The number of protons in an atom is that element's atomic number.

The periodic table lists the known elements. It includes each element's symbol and atomic number. There are 118 known chemical elements on Earth. Most are found in nature. Some are made in laboratories.

Russian scientist Dmitri Mendeleyev created the periodic table of elements in 1871.

All natural elements came from space. The first elements were created during the big bang more than 13 billion years ago. The big bang theory explains how the universe began. It started at a single point. Then it began growing outward. Today, the universe continues to grow bigger and bigger.

Scientists believe the first elements were hydrogen, helium, lithium, and beryllium. Gravity caused clouds of these elements to form stars and **galaxies**. Then, other natural elements were created within the stars.

COMBINING ELEMENTS

Elements can combine to make compounds. There are close to 1 million known compounds. For example, water is a compound. It is made of the elements hydrogen and oxygen. Compounds can combine to make mixtures.

A compound or mixture can exist in different states. They are called states of matter. The three main states

Water is a compound that is necessary for life.

of matter are solids, liquids, and gases. In each state, the atoms act differently.

In solids, the atoms are packed together tightly. They have a strong attraction to one another. They can only move a little.

In liquids, more space exists between atoms. They are still somewhat attracted to one another, but they can move around.

In gases, there is a lot of space between atoms. They move freely. They have a very weak attraction to one another.

ATOMS IN MATTER

ATOMS IN A SOLID

ATOMS IN A LIQUID

ATOMS IN A GAS

SUPER SOLIDS

There are many solids in outer space. In space, dust **swirls** around new stars. This dust gathers and **compacts** over millions of years. It forms solid rocks. Planets form when many rocks press together.

Balloons are solids, but the helium inside is a gas.

All the planets in our solar system, including Saturn, were formed when space dust compacted together.

A solid has certain qualities that are different from other states of matter. A solid has a definite shape that is not easy to change. This is because its atoms are linked tightly together. But all solids aren't the same.

Some solids are malleable. That means they can bend without breaking. Many metals are malleable. Other solids, such as glass, are not malleable. If you try to bend them, they just break into smaller pieces.

Some solids can be stretched. Copper is often stretched to make wire. Rubber is another stretchable solid. It is used in tires and balloons.

The strongest solids are very difficult to break. Steel and concrete are very strong solids. That's why they are good for making buildings and bridges.

CHAOTIC GASES

Our planet has layers of gas around it. The layers make up our atmosphere. The atmosphere traps the air we breathe. It provides our weather. It also protects Earth from the sun and **meteorites**.

The planet Jupiter is made mainly of gas but has a solid core.

Some planets form as gas giants. These are planets that are mostly atmosphere with little surface. They are farther from the sun than planets made mostly of rock are.

Jupiter is one gas giant in our solar system. It is made of mostly hydrogen and helium. Scientists believe its small **core** is a mix of the metals iron and nickel.

Most kinds of gas are **invisible**. Gas has no fixed shape or volume. It can squeeze into small spaces. And it takes on the shape of its container. Its atoms act very differently than those in solids.

Gas atoms move in all directions. They hit other gas atoms and the sides of the container. At higher temperatures, the atoms move even faster.

In space, no containers hold gases in a certain spot. So why does an atmosphere stay in place? A planet's gravity keeps the gases near the planet's surface. This force pulls the atmosphere toward a planet's **core**.

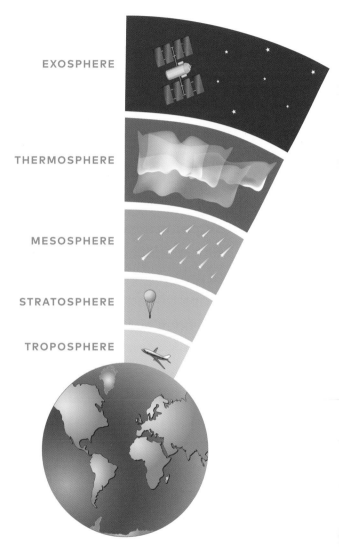

EXOSPHERE

THERMOSPHERE

MESOSPHERE

STRATOSPHERE

TROPOSPHERE

Earth's atmosphere is divided into five layers. Without the atmosphere, our planet could not support life.

15

FLOWING
LIQUIDS

Water is necessary for life on Earth. Nearly two-thirds of our planet's surface is water. Many scientists believe life first began in Earth's oceans. And the human body is also mostly made of water.

Earth has so much water because it is just the right distance from the sun. It doesn't get too hot or too cold. It is just right. That's why scientists call Earth's distance from the sun the Goldilocks Zone.

Oceans contain 96 percent of Earth's water.

When water gets cold enough, its atoms condense and it becomes a solid.

Liquid is a state of matter between solid and gas. It has some qualities of each. A liquid's atoms are not as tightly arranged as a solid's. But like a solid, a liquid has a fixed volume. And it is difficult to compress.

However, a liquid's atoms are more ordered than a gas's. But like a gas, it takes on the shape of its container.

Two general types of liquids exist. There are pure liquids, such as water. And there are liquid mixtures. The ocean is a mixture of salt and water.

EXTREME
STATES

There are **two states of matter in addition to solid, liquid, and gas.** They are rarely found naturally on Earth. These states are plasma and Bose-Einstein condensate (BEC).

Plasma is an extremely hot gas. Most matter in the universe is plasma. It's found in and between stars. Lightning and glowing **auroras** are also made of plasma.

Aurora borealis occurs when plasma from the sun hits Earth's magnetic field. Aurora borealis is also called northern lights.

A BEC exists at the coldest temperature possible. This is called absolute zero. Gas cooled to absolute zero changes. Its atoms slow down. They clump together and can't move separately.

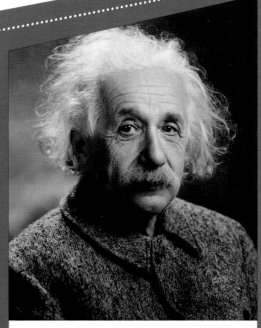

Albert Einstein

Satyendra Nath Bose

BEC is named after scientists Satyendra Nath Bose and Albert Einstein. In the early 1920s, Bose was working on a theory of small particles. He **collaborated** with Einstein.

They **predicted** the BEC in 1924. But the **technology** at the time could not create the temperature of absolute zero. So Bose and Einstein could not prove their theory. In 1995, scientists at the University of Colorado could. They were able to get a gas cold enough to make a BEC.

CONSERVATION
OF MATTER

Stars are born throughout the universe. Each star exists for billions of years. Then it eventually collapses. After collapsing, some stars explode.

After a star explodes, it leaves behind dust and gas. The dust and gas **swirl** together. They will become part of a new star.

Like stars, all matter in the universe recycles itself. It never disappears. It just changes form. This is the conservation of matter.

Chemical **reactions** change matter to other forms. The reactions change the matter's chemical elements. They reform into different elements. Burning wood

A star's explosion is known as a supernova.

When you roast marshmallows over a campfire, you are watching matter change form.

is a chemical **reaction**. The fire adds heat energy and oxygen to the wood. The result is **carbon dioxide**, steam, and ash.

Temperature and pressure cause atoms to slow down, speed up, or compress. This changes matter into other states. For example, a heated solid can become a liquid. Or a heated liquid can change to a gas. Some heated solids can even change directly to gases.

CHANGING STATES

It takes energy to make change happen. Solid ice can melt to become liquid water. To become a solid again, it must be refrozen. These changes are caused by adding or removing heat energy.

Adding heat energy makes a solid's atoms and molecules move faster. The solid's temperature increases. It reaches its melting point. This temperature depends on the material. For water, the melting point is 32 degrees Fahrenheit (0°C). The metal iron melts at a much higher temperature. Its melting point is 2,750 degrees Fahrenheit (1,510°C).

Icicles form when dripping water freezes, melts, and refreezes.

When magma reaches Earth's surface, it is called lava.

High temperatures and extreme pressure melt metal and rock deep under Earth's surface. This liquid metal and rock is called **magma**. It can escape to Earth's surface through volcanoes.

Take away heat energy and a liquid freezes. Its atoms and molecules slow down. The liquid becomes a solid at its freezing point.

MOVING GASES

The more heat is added to a liquid, the more the liquid's atoms and molecules move. Soon the liquid reaches its boiling point. This is when it becomes a gas. The atoms and molecules break their bonds to each other. When water boils, the gas it changes to is called steam.

In some places, boiling water and steam shoot out of the earth in geysers.

Changing to a gas is also how water reaches Earth's atmosphere. This is a very important part of the water **cycle**. As the sun heats the Earth, water **evaporates** from lakes, rivers, and oceans. It becomes a gas and rises into the atmosphere.

Instead of melting, dry ice turns directly to a gas as it warms up.

In colder temperatures, gases turn back to liquids. This is called **condensation**. It forms clouds high in the sky. Temperatures are much lower there. Condensation also causes fog closer to the ground. Clouds release their water as rain, snow, sleet, or hail. The water returns to Earth's surface and begins the cycle again.

Sometimes solids change directly into gases. This is called sublimation. Dry ice is frozen **carbon dioxide**. It turns into a gas when heated. In nature, snow or ice can become gas in certain areas. On tall mountains, cold temperatures, high winds, strong sunlight, and low air pressure can cause sublimation.

MATTER
MATTERS

Take a look around. Matter is everywhere. You can't miss it. It's found in everything from the stars in the sky to specks of dust on Earth. It just comes in different

The Crab Nebula in the constellation Taurus

combinations of elements. Matter exists in different states. Liquid water fills Earth's oceans. Solids form Earth's rocky land. Gases fill our skies and churn deep in space. A nebula gives birth to stars made of plasma. Scientists can even create the BEC state in laboratories.

Whatever its state, matter is made of atoms and molecules. Their movement, slow or fast, changes matter. Heat energy and pressure make matter change from state to state too.

Matter moves constantly. It changes from one form to another. Stars burn brightly for billions of years. Their deaths feed the **cycle**, helping new stars form. It's this matter, born in space, which makes life possible on Earth.

Matter is in plants and trees. Even you are made of matter!

GASSED-UP BALLOON

AN EXPERIMENT WITH STATES OF MATTER

QUESTION

Can you fill a balloon without blowing into it?

RESEARCH

You have learned that liquid and gas are two states of matter (page 11). It's also possible for a gas to be **dissolved** in a liquid. What happens when the gas is released? Here's what you'll need to find out:

- large bottle of soda
- balloon
- stopwatch or clock

PREDICT

Read the steps below. Make a guess about what will happen. **Predict** how opening the bottle will affect the balloon. Write your prediction down.

TEST

1. Open the bottle. What do you hear? There is **carbon dioxide** gas in the soda. That's what makes the hissing sound.

2. Stretch a balloon over the top of the bottle. Start the stopwatch.

3. Watch the balloon. Keep checking for changes.

4. What happens? How long does it take to start changing? How long until it stops changing?

ASSESS

Was your prediction correct? Why or why not? What would happen if you used a larger or smaller bottle of soda? Or a larger or smaller balloon? Try it and find out!

GLOSSARY

aurora – light in the sky in Earth's northern hemisphere caused by atoms moving along the planet's magnetic field.

carbon dioxide – a heavy, colorless gas that is formed when fuel containing the element carbon is burned.

collaborate – to work with another person or group in order to do something or reach a goal.

compact – to press together.

condensation – to change from a gas or a vapor into a liquid or a solid. This is usually caused by a decrease in temperature.

core – the center of a space object such as a planet, moon, or star.

cycle – a period of time or a complete process that repeats itself.

dissolve – to pass into solution or become liquid.

evaporate – to change from a liquid or a solid into a vapor.

galaxy – a very large group of stars, planets and other objects in space. The Earth is in a galaxy called the Milky Way.

invisible – unable to be seen.

magma – melted rock beneath Earth's surface.

meteorite – a space object that hits the surface of the earth.

predict – to guess something ahead of time on the basis of observation, experience, or reasoning.

reaction – the chemical action of two or more substances on each other. This produces at least one additional substance.

swirl – to whirl or to move smoothly in circles.

technology – the use of science in solving problems.

WEBSITES

To learn more about Science in Action, visit **booklinks.abdopublishing.com.** These links are routinely monitored and updated to provide the most current information available.

INDEX